MW01100790

Three Green Rats
An Eco Tale

For ages 7 to 11 and precocious adults

Also by Linda Mason Hunter

The Healthy Home: An Attic-To-Basement Guide to Toxin-Free Living

Southwest Style: A Home-Lover's Guide to Architecture and Design

Creating a Safe and Healthy Home

Green Clean (with Mikki Halpin)

Three Green Rats
An Eco Tale

By Linda Mason Hunter and Suzanne Summersgill

Illustrated by Suzanne Summersgill

First Edition

HunterInk@PinnStudio

Vancouver, British Columbia

First in a series

First Edition

Published by HunterInk@PinnStudio
Vancouver, British Columbia
www.threegreenrats.com

Library and Archives Canada Cataloguing in Publication

Hunter, Linda Mason
Three green rats : an eco tale / Linda Mason Hunter,
Suzanne Summersgill.

ISBN 978-0-9881393-0-5

I. Summersgill, Suzanne II. Title.

PS3608.U5943T47 2012   j813'.6   C2012-905662-6

JUVENILE FICTION/Nature & the Natural World/General (see
also headings under Animals)
JUVENILE FICTION/Readers/Chapter Books
JUVENILE FICTION/Nature & the Natural World/Environment

Book design by Joline Rivera, idesign, inc.
Cover by Jacqueline Wang

Printed in Canada

For Ellie Marie
      --- LMH

For my grandchildren
who will walk on earth one day
      --- SES

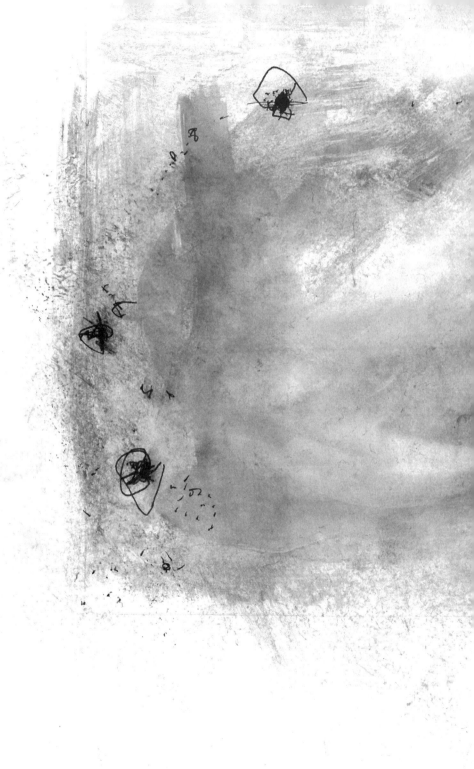

Walk softly

Preface

Born in the Year of the Rat

T he Chinese zodiac is divided into twelve sections. Each section represents a year and is symbolized by a creature. Rat is the first in the cycle and represents earth, a time of renewal.

People born in the Year of the Rat take on rodent-like characteristics. They are enterprising and resourceful, witty and cunning, and above all steadfastly thrifty. They work hard, are clever at adapting to their environment, and are born leaders who don't give a snicker what others think—all useful qualities if we are to get down to business and clean up our planet. Most rats have generous sunny dispositions, making them fun friends to hang with.

That's our pack o rats, alright! Easy-going Oliver (the youngest) never buys a thing. Wilbur (the middle brother) is a master of clever reuse. Older brother Tom tends the most prolific garden in the province. Together they set out to live a simple life and end up changing the world. This is their tale.

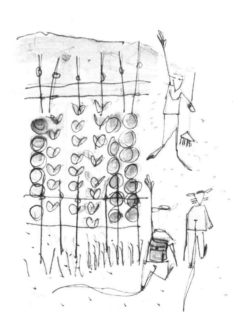

Table of Contents

Not so long ago,

in the land of

Here and Now...

...Tintown was a dirty, noisy place: planes roaring, buses hooting, taxis tooting, sirens screaming. Big idling cars jammed the highways, each carrying a single impatient driver.

All earth sounds got lost in the din. The music of wee birds, whistling wind, rustling leaves, rushing water became so very hard to hear. All the dirt, smoke, and gassy pollution made the air feel exhausted, thick, and lumpy, like a cloud of bad gravy.

Walls of trash lined backstreets and alleys. Mountains of rubbish buried once-happy playgrounds. Filth slicked the sidewalks.

Tintowners didn't care a hoot. They hurried and scurried about and didn't think about the mess they made at all.

1
Uppity Ethel Misrington

Mrs. Ethel Misrington didn't mind the smell of truck exhaust and factory smokestacks. "That's the smell of money being made," she said rubbing her bony ol' paws together. And she loved the sound of racing traffic. "It's the sound of business roaring like a Jaguar to the nearest ATM," she chuckled greedily.

Ethel was the richest rat in town. She had more money than the queen. If you asked any rat "Who runs Tintown?" they'd reply, "Why Mrs. Ethel Misrington, of course!"

She lived in a fancy house stuffed with all the latest gadgets. If it plugged in, she had it:

- air conditioners and space heaters
- hairdryers and hot rollers
- toaster ovens, convection ovens, microwave ovens
- crepe makers
- waffle grids
- blenders
- steamers
- ice cream machines

She even had an alarm clock that brewed coffee, played music, and turned on the shower. She had the latest-model clothes dryer tumbling away in her laundry room, for she wouldn't be caught dead hanging her clothes out on a line to dry.

"I don't want neighbors seeing my underthings," she sniffed. "It's downright indecent!"

Everything in Mrs. Misrington's universe was perfect except for a trio of pesky bees

perpetually buzzing around her lacquered hairdo. They annoyed her as much as the three-pack of brothers who lived at the end of Broken Bottle Lane.

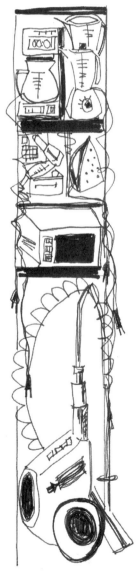

"Those three Green brothers make me so mad I could spit! I don't like them one single bit! They are a windmilling, compost-churning, dumpster-diving nuisance," Ethel grumbled to herself day in and day out, for the very thought of them made her tremble with annoyance.

What nagged at Ethel like a burr in her underpants was how the brothers lived so happily without shopping at her store. Every other rat in town shopped there.

"It's the lifeblood of the Tintown economy!" she crowed to anyone who would listen.

"Those ragamuffin boys don't belong in Tintown," she harrumphed to her grand-niece over breakfast one morning. "They don't buy a thing—not food at my grocery store, not gas at my gas station, not electricity from my power plant—not so much as *The Tintown Daily News.*"

Ethel Misrington had big plans for her empire. She wanted to build Tintown's first Super Duper Big Box Rat Mart right at the end of Broken Bottle Lane. "It'll revitalize the whole area, create jobs, be good for business," she whispered into the mayor's ear and the ears of the Tintown Town Council.

But the three odd Green brothers with their crazy ideas threatened her plan. If everyone lived as they did, no one would ever shop at Rat Mart. "I'll put a stick in their bicycle spokes," Mrs. Misrington vowed to herself each night before going to sleep.

2
Mischief

On the edge of Tintown, right down Broken Bottle Lane, lived a mischief of rats in a neat compact hut made of foraged bits and pieces. They were a wholesome threesome, by and large, except for a tinge of green about their thumbs. While ordinary rats mindlessly skittered around eating junk, tossing out wrappers, and buying Rat Mart items they didn't need or want, Oliver, Wilbur, and Tom Green lived simply, never taking more than they needed to survive.

Everything they needed they made. They spent almost nothing and reused everything—even grimy dishwater and vegetable peels! Instead of gas-powered cars, they pedaled

around town on bicycles cobbled together from pipes and parts from the perfectly good lawnmowers, clocks, and wheelbarrows other Tintowners threw away.

They grew their own food and stored it for the winter. They watered their garden with rainwater from a cistern Oliver dug in the ground. And they diligently stored every drop of used washwater in a grey-water tank next to the garden.

Freeways and parking lots had covered over Tintown's streams and rivers long ago, but the brothers still had a clear freshwater pond on their patch. In a town so dry your nostrils sometimes stuck together, the Greens had all the water they needed with enough left over to fill the birdbath.

While Oli, Will, and Tom were cheerful (mostly) and full of life, other rats in Tintown scurried about perpetually dissatisfied. No matter how many new things they bought, they complained and grumbled and found fault with each other all day long. Nothing made them happy, least of all the three unconventional orphans living at the end of Broken Bottle Lane.

Oliver particularly annoyed them.

"He smells as ripe as old cheese," they snickered behind his back. It was true.

Oli couldn't stand the idea of wasting good clean water on a bath. He got so stinky skunks crossed the road to avoid him.

"Peeyew!" squealed Mrs. Ethel Misrington when she found him grubbing in garbage cans. She pinched her nose with one manicured paw, grabbed hold of her grand-niece with the other, and hurriedly crossed to the other side of the lane.

When the odor got to be too much for even Will and Tom, one of them would say, "Oliver, I made soap this morning. It's officially 'Get Clean Day.'" Sometimes Oli got the hint, but sometimes Will and Tom just picked him up and threw him in the pond.

Oli's strengths weren't limited to his smell. Every morning, he haunted the alleys hunting for junk and looking for trash that still had some use left in it.

Where others saw junk Oli saw treasure—pieces of wire and shreds of fuzz, broken-down toys and springs and things—which he added to his large pile of Found Things located just outside the gate to their patch. Oliver considered this a public service and posted a sign saying:

FREE.
Every Rat Welcome
Take what you want

Canny rats willing to dig could take home anything from a trombone to a perfectly serviceable scooter that cost five dollars at Rat Mart.

"That pile of junk is an eyesore," growled Mrs. Misrington, stopping to glare. When her niece picked up the handle of a rusty red wagon, Ethel hollered, "Maybelline! Put that thing down. It's filthy!"

Oli had a particular fondness for collecting garden hose. Every last bit he brought back from his prowls he duct-taped together until he had enough to stretch nearly to the end of Broken Bottle Lane.

"Hey, bro, we don't need any more hose," Will told him at least once a week.

"It might come in handy one day," Oliver replied mildly.

Tintowners made mean comments about Wilbur too.

"He's a strange bird," most said sourly, shaking their heads.

"That riff-rat thinks he's better than the rest of us," Mrs. Misrington sneered through her carefully coifed whiskers. She intended to laugh in a superior way, but it came out as a messy, sniggery sneeze.

"Goodness, my allergies!" she sniffed, dabbing her snout with a hankie.

In fact, Mrs. Ethel Misrington was right. Wilbur did fancy himself a cut above the average rat. He was so wrapped up inventing contraptions that "hello" and "goodbye" were all he bothered to say to his neighbors. It scandalized Ethel each time Will passed her in the lane without even saying "Good day."

"Downright rude!" she exclaimed, hurrying little Maybelline along.

Wilbur had a gift for invention and fanciful design. As a wee ratling, he was always making something amazing from junk: a cape made from raggedy sweaters thrown in the trash, wind catchers from broken-down toys. He took wheels from cars and heads from dolls, sprockets from gadgets and torn overalls, a bit from here, a piece from there, and he made one-of-a-kind objects of curiosity and wonder, far better than the sum of their parts.

Gentle Tom, the gardener of the family, spoke little and went into town less. Content to putter around the patch, he whistled while he worked, nurturing the land the way his grandfather taught him. He saved seeds from last year's harvest and caught rain in a big oak barrel.

Instead of buying bags of chemicals from Rat Mart's gardening center, Tom maintained a magnificent drug-free compost heap. Vegetable and fruit scraps made their way to the pile, as did old newspapers and autumn leaves. He watered the heap and turned it often. Gradually the mess transformed itself into dark, crumbly, nutrient-rich humus—gardener's gold.

Maybe it had nothing to do with the garden's success, but when he tended the pile Tom never failed to sing his grandpa's compost song:

Cantaloupe and melon rind,
Rotten veg and moldy grime,
Little twigs and dried-up plants,
Wood chips and torn underpants.
Oo la la, oo la la

New-mown grass and autumn leaves,
Magazines and plaid-shirt sleeves,
Wet cardboard and clipped toenails,
Crumpled napkins, shells from snails.
Oo la lay, oo la lay

Fruit skins and dried pea pods,
Fish bones and weedy clods,
Teabags and cabbage leaves,
Eggshells and fresh seaweed.
Oh oola, oola, oola lay

Everything will die one day
There is no life without decay
So to the earth from whence you came
To rot, break down, and green again.
Oh oola, oola, oola lay

Every summer, Tom's garden won first place in the Tintown Garden Club Contest, and his big juicy tomatoes won blue ribbons at the Tin County Fair. Though Mrs. Ethel Misrington usually took the prize for "Best Looking Tomato," Tom always won first place for "Tastiest Tomato."

Every
Single
Year

This fueled Mrs. Misrington's dislike, for even though she lavished gallons of chemical fertilizer and so much pesticide on her garden that no bug dared go near it, flowers were afraid to bloom, and her tomatoes tasted like sawdust.

3
Maybelline

Mrs. Ethel Misrington did not have a green thumb. Perhaps it was because she desperately tried to force things into the shapes she wanted rather than simply letting them be. It wasn't just her tomatoes that didn't thrive—her roses drooped, her dahlias pooped, her sweet peas listed, and the leaves of parched daisies curled in on themselves in sadness.

Most every afternoon, she could be found standing in her garden in a big straw hat and gardening gloves, leaning on her rake, sniffling and sneezing into her sleeve. She couldn't understand why her flowers were so uncooperative, including that spindly bud living at the very top of her house: a tiny ratling who would not grow. No matter how many vitamin-enriched processed products Mrs. M plied her with, her grand-niece, Maybelline, remained small, pale, and very, very quiet.

Maybelline Burlingame Helena Stu hadn't laughed once since coming to live with "Auntie Miserable." In fact, she barely spoke at all and clung to her tail as if it were her only lifeline. When no one was looking, she raised it to her face and stroked the soft tuft at the tip against her cheek for comfort.

Mrs. Ethel Misrington was always busy running to and fro, shuffling papers, checking her stocks, writing to her banker, scheming with the mayor on the telephone. If Maybelline happened to drift into the room, her aunt would snap, "Not now, child. Can't you see I'm busy?" and the timid ratling would retreat back to her hidey hole.

Next time Mrs. M looked over her glasses, she was relieved to not see the stubbornly ungrowing child—a reminder of the obstinacy of all living things.

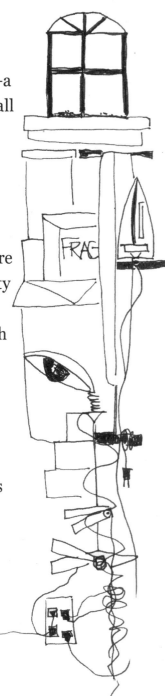

Maybelline squirreled herself away in the attic atop Mrs. Misrington's house where the grimy windows were too high to clean and the dusty boxes made her nose tickle.

"Auntie Ethel has too much stuff," she said to no one in particular.

A hodgepodge of stuff filled the attic: ragged folders of yellowing papers, piles of catalogues, broken appliances that couldn't be fixed or that cost more to repair than to replace. Among Maybelline's many discoveries were:

- bug traps
- a chocolate fountain that gurgled emptily
- an electric clipper for unwanted tail hair
- whisker irons that gave her a nasty shock
- a contraption for perking up your ears while you slept
- a clap lamp that went on but wouldn't go off again no matter how hard she clapped
- and a collection of rubber stamps with backwards words.

When she held the stamps up to a cobwebby mirror, she could read words like "foreclosed," "final payment due," "request denied," and (curiously) one with the letters EM+ MB enclosed in a heart. Maybelline liked hearts so she wet a dried-up stamp pad with her spit and stamped the heart with the mysterious letters everywhere.

One morning, while studying the financial news over breakfast, Mrs. M realized it had been some time since she'd seen her grand-niece. She took off her glasses. "Where is that disappearing child? She's more like a ghost than any relative of mine." Then she shouted, "*Maybelline Burlingame Helena Stu!*"

"I'm right here, Aunt," came a small voice from beneath the table.

"Stand up, child. Stop slouching."

"I am standing." Maybelline was so small that only the tips of her ears appeared above the tabletop. The chairs were too high for her to climb up on, so she perched on an empty tin of Deluxe Cookie Selection while nibbling on a bowl of vitamin-enriched, cocoa-puffed Crunch-a-Bunch cereal she held in her hand.

"What in heaven's name are you doing under the table?" Mrs. M sneezed in frustration. She wanted nothing more than for Maybelline to grow into the very model of

herself, but how could this shrinking violet ever run a retail empire?

Mrs. M sneezed and was about to turn back to her newspaper when a movement from outside caught her eye. She turned to the window. Through the smog, she spotted a flicker among the treetops above the Greens' patch.

"What in tarnation are those foolish  boys doing now?" Mrs. M reached for her binoculars. "BAT HOUSES! They're putting up BAT HOUSES! I *HATE* bats!"

When Maybelline heard the word "bat," something stirred inside her.

"Bat houses?" she whispered.

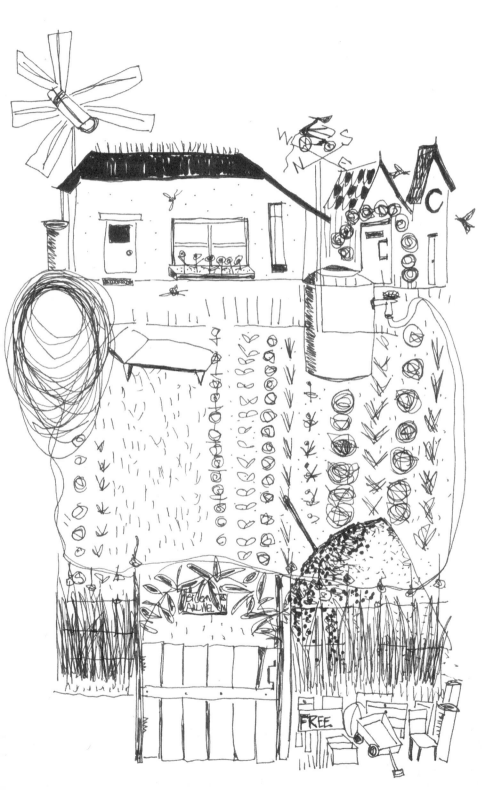

4

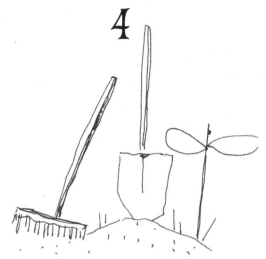

Every Shade of Green

L ater that morning, she drifted unnoticed,
pale as dandelion fuzz, out the door and
along the lane.

The air was stale and grey. "Tintown Grey,"
locals called it. Maybelline tiptoed down the
slippery alley, past flat tires and rusty paint
cans, past asphalt lawns and the occasional
weed poking up through cement, past green
plastic garbage bags lining the lane like
ornamental hedges.

The putrid smell of rotting garbage wafted into her nostrils.

Sniff. Sniff.

Sure enough, it smelled like home.

Rats raced by on their way to jobs in factories, offices, and stores. She could hear the muffled rhythmic thumps of massive machinery in a nearby factory and the roar of traffic hurtling down the highway and overpasses. Suddenly, a cloud of car exhaust obscured her vision, and for a moment she was lost.

When the choking haze cleared a bit, she found herself standing outside the dense, crazily woven fence of latticework and brambles that surrounded the Green brothers' patch. She looked up, and had to lean way back on her heels to see the tippy tops of towering cottonwoods and oaks that seemed to wave even higher than the jumble of warehouses and high-rises.

She tried to peek through the fence, but it was too tightly woven and sprouting with leaves. She could hear little animals peeping and scurrying around inside.

"*Eeeeks!*" she yelped, jumping back with alarm. "This fence is alive!"

A little further down the lane, she spied Oli's heap of Found Things next to an arched opening with a wooden gate and a hand-painted sign that read:

Green Brothers'
Patch and Recycling Depot
All Welcome

The latch was too high for Maybelline to reach, but when she crouched down she could see inside.

"It's so green!" she gasped, letting go of her tail in surprise. She'd never seen such beautiful disorder. Every imaginable shade of green startled her eyes—from emerald to shimmering chartreuse. The air smelled fresh and delicious and seemed to sparkle.

She stood gawking.

In the corner stood a tidy shed covered in climbing red roses. She watched a swallow dart under the eave then dart quickly back out again, quick as a flutter. When she spied the pivoting weathervane atop the roof, in the shape of a rat

cycling madly in the breeze, she smiled.

Sunlight dappled the property with warm places and shady nooks. Bumble bees buzzed happily among the wildflowers, cottontail bunnies hopped about, and a garter snake slithered into the woodpile. There was a lush garden with teepees of beans and peas, trellises dripping with berries, and a rambling squash patch.

And trees—tall leafy trees stretching their limbs to the sky! Maybelline had never stood in the center of such a huge mass of rustling leaves, and the sight and sound of them gave her goosebumps.

She wandered toward a pond ashimmer with violet, green, and blue lights that turned out to be dragonflies dancing above the water. Kneeling on a big stone at the edge, she watched with delight as silver fish nuzzled plants waving like hula dancers under water. Her mind was adazzle with so much to see.

And so much to hear! Birds singing, insects

chirping, owls hooting. Even the compost heap burped and farted almost imperceptibly. A breeze rustled through Maybelline's hair and she smiled.

"Ahem," a soft voice spoke behind her. Maybelline nearly leapt out of her skin. Reaching for her tail, she glanced up at a tall gangly rat in dirty overalls with wild tufts of hair.

"Whoa, careful. You'll scare Martha." He nodded towards a weird stick creature perched on his weathered paw.

"Ooooo, a bug!" she shrank back. "My aunt says bugs put stings on you and infestigate."

The wild-haired rat looked as if he might laugh, but was too polite. "Martha is a praying mantis," he explained. "She and her babies only eat the bugs that chomp on my lettuce and onions. She won't harm you...Wait! I'm forgetting my manners." He gently guided Martha onto his shoulder then held out a weathered paw with soil-

45

blackened claws. "Tom Green," he offered.

Maybelline held tight to her tail, silent and terrified.

"And you are," he coaxed gently.

"Maybelline Burlingame Helena Stu," she quavered.

Tom laughed. "That's a big name for a rat like you."

Just then, the gate banged open and a bespeckled rat boinked in on his HopRod.

"Close the gate, Will," Tom yelled.

"Oli's right behind me," the rat on the hopper yelled back.

Sure enough, the selfsame rat her aunt had yelled "Peeyew!" at pedaled in pulling a trailer piled high with junk. Oli braked directly in front of Maybelline, and with a big smile, asked bluntly, "Where you from?"

Boink

Boink

Boink

"My name is Maybelline Burlingame Helena Stu. I've come from across town to live with my Auntie Ethel Misrington. My parents had uh..... an unfortunate accident." She lowered her eyes and stared at her feet.

"Caught in a trap, thumped by a broom, or poisoned by pesticides?" Oli asked rather callously.

"Caught in a trap," Maybelline swallowed hard.

"Ooooo," Oli declared. "That's tough. Our Mum got beaten to a pulp with a toilet plunger."

"What's it like living with the richest rat in town?" Wilbur hastily changed the subject.

Maybelline shrugged.

"Your aunt doesn't like us much," Tom offered.

"How 'bout we just call you Maybee?" Oli asked her.

Maybelline nodded, then whispering an abrupt "goodbye" ran to the gate, slid underneath, and sprinted lickety split straight back to her aunt's house.

5
Reduce. Reuse.
Recycle.

Maybelline awoke with a stretch and a smile and hurried down the three flights of stairs to breakfast. She found Mrs. Misrington up to her whiskers in newspapers and hollering on her phone. Maybee approached the table, bid her aunt a respectful "good morning," and was startled to realize that her chin was level with the tabletop when the day before she was standing under it!

"That's strange," she squeaked.

"Speak up, child!" snarled Mrs M slamming down the phone.

"I said, 'That's strange.'"

"What's strange?"

"I seem to be a bit bigger."

"I should certainly hope so with all I'm feeding you! Now run along! Can't you see I'm busy?"

"Yes, Auntie Ethel," Maybee muttered, grabbing a box of Jumbleyoos ultra-processed fruit-like juice before heading out the door and down the lane to the Green brothers' patch.

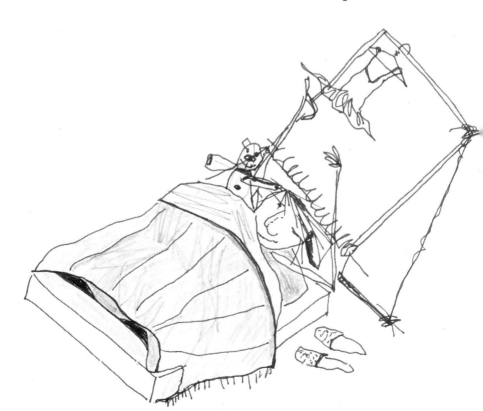

"Look who's here," Will called soon as he saw her.

"Happy to see you, Maybee Stu," Tom said, offering his dirty paw in welcome.

Maybee shook it this time, smiling shyly.

"How about a tour of the patch, Maybee?" Wilbur suggested.

Maybelline didn't need to be asked twice.

"What's that big tank for?" she questioned, pointing to a grey whale of thing standing next to the garden.

"That's our grey-water tank," Oli said proudly. "We save used washwater and store it there."

"You save your bath water?" Maybee asked, appalled.

"Yep! Laundry and dishwasher too. Every drop," he replied.

"What for?"

"For watering the garden and washing the grime off our boots and bicycles. That way we don't waste precious drinking water," Oli explained.

"It looks to me like you don't pay for much of anything. Everything here is used or reused," Maybee giggled. "What's that?" she asked, pointing to a tall spinning thing in the middle of the patch.

"That's our windmill generator," answered Wilbur. "It supplies all the electricity three rats need, which isn't much."

Maybee twirled around looking for another curiosity. "What's that?" she asked, pointing to a crooked hut with a half moon carved in the door.

"That's our composting outhouse. You've got to try it!" Wilbur urged.

"Ummmmm. I beg your pardon." Maybee had never been so embarrassed in her life. But curiosity overcame her reluctance and she followed Wilbur to have a look.

"Oh my!" she gasped. Before her stood a throne with a high upholstered back, armrests, and cushy seat. It was unlike any toilet she had ever seen. A bucket of sawdust stood beside it, along with a step stool for climbing up.

"It's not stinky!" Maybee sniffed. In fact, it smelled a bit like the lavender bush growing outside the door.

"And it doesn't use a drop of water," Will boasted.

"How can it work then?" she asked, despite herself.

"When you've done your business, you toss a cup of sawdust on top. Easy as poo. No muss, no fuss. In a few month's time it all goes on the flower garden. Makes great organic fertilizer."

"*Eew!*"

"This way." Wilbur wheeled around and strode off so fast Maybee had to run to keep up.

"This is my pride and joy," he said, pointing to three golden panels glittering in the center of a tidy workshop.

"*Wow!*" Maybee declared.

"Look here." Will pointed to a winding line in the mosaic of glinting squares on the surface of each panel. On closer look, Maybee realized that each piece was a bit of glass bottle; she could still see parts of letters and logos on some of them.

"These tiny pieces are in the exact same formation as the spirals of sunflower seeds. They capture the sun's heat and turn it into electricity to heat our water."

At that moment, Tom appeared in the doorway. "You guys hungry?" he asked. "Oliver is making crusty cricket buns for lunch."

"Mmm, crickets," Maybee answered right away for they were her favorite.

Over cricket buns, carrot nibbles, and the best tomato she'd ever tasted, Maybee became friends with Oliver, Wilbur, and Tom Green.

As they cleared the table, Oli told her his secrets for storing food without refrigeration. She learned that the freshness of eggs can be tested in water:  the fresher they are, the further they sink. She learned that putting apples in the same storage bin as potatoes keeps potatoes from sprouting and that keeping root vegetables in a vertical position allows them to stay fresh longer.

Tom showed her how to turn the compost and dig up weeds, mulch the garden and plant seeds. He showed her how to unwind the garden hose and where the faucet was located on the grey-water tank. He taught her that bees pollinate flowers and that crops can't grow without them.

Maybee spent the rest of the afternoon sitting beside Tom in the soft garden dirt. His tools were too big for her hands, so Wilbur whipped up a pint-sized spade and a rake in his workshop. Neither talked much as both were quiet by nature, choosing instead to work side by side in companionable silence. As she gardened,

Maybee cherished the smells, the warmth of the sun, the plants growing strong. At the end of the day, Tom was surprised that such a small ratling could work so hard and so steadily without giving up.

At dusk, she watched lovely bats fly in and out of their house high on a pole. She learned that a single bat can eat one thousand mosquitoes in an hour. The brothers seemed to know everything!

After a supper of beet stew and fresh garden lettuces, with strawberries and cream for dessert, the shadows grew long and Maybee knew it was time to go home.

"I better get going. I might be in trouble. Thanks! It's been a great day."

"I'll whiz you home on my bike," Will offered.

Every window was lit when they pulled up in front of Mrs. Misrington's house, but the brightness did nothing to cheer up the place. Maybee climbed down from the bike's basket and waved Will goodbye.

Once inside, she went from room to room turning off lights until she came to the study. There she found her aunt fast asleep, her snores sounding like a truckload of marbles rumbling down the highway, her head on her keyboard, the computer screen filled with line after line of the letter k.

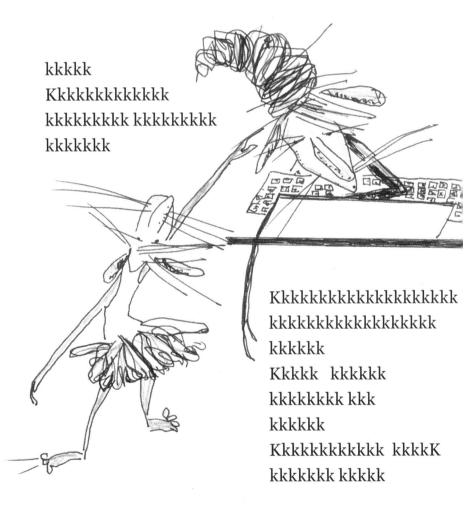

kkkkk
Kkkkkkkkkkkk
kkkkkkkkk kkkkkkkkk
kkkkkkk

Kkkkkkkkkkkkkkkkkkkkk
kkkkkkkkkkkkkkkkkk
kkkkkk
Kkkkk kkkkkk
kkkkkkkk kkk
kkkkkk
Kkkkkkkkkkkk kkkkK
kkkkkkk kkkkk

When Maybee tapped her shoulder, Mrs. M jumped awake, sneezing violently. "What are you still doing up? Off to bed! Nighty night-night."

As Maybee tucked herself in, she didn't feel quite as lonely as she felt the night before. She hugged her ted and drifted into a sweet green sleep filled with peeping animals, whirling whirligigs, timid Martha, and three cheerfully eccentric orphans.

6

A Fearful Mood

The next morning found Mrs. Misrington in a fearful mood. Sneezing had kept her awake all night. Her beady eyes were red and blurry, and her nose was chapped from so much horn blowing.

Normally, when her aunt was in a wretched mood, Maybelline didn't say boo. Whenever

she heard "Maybelline Burlingame Helena Stu!" she hid in a closet until the storm passed. But today was different. Instead of hiding from her aunt's foul mood, she continued to giggle over the comics section of the morning newspaper.

The tips of Maybee's ears and snout were flushed with pink, and she actually wolfed down her cereal instead of nibbling little bits.

She stood on a footstool instead of a Deluxe Cookie Selection tin as she was suddenly quite a bit bigger.

Regarding her niece warily, Mrs. M poured herself a cup of coffee and cracked her newspaper. After a particularly violent sneezing fit, she reached for her binoculars in search of something to complain about.

"*Bat houses*! Those fools are still at it. I'm going to put a stop to this!"

She picked up her purse, jammed her hat on her head, and grabbed

Maybee's arm. "Maybelline, you're about to get a lesson in leadership."

Auntie Ethel achooed all the way down Broken Bottle Lane, yanking Maybelline behind her like a sack of potatoes. By the time they reached the Green's gate, Tintown's richest rat was wheezing and sneezing and perspiring alarmingly.

"Maybelline," she groaned, "I need to sit down. I believe I'm having one of my spells."

"Come sit in here, Auntie Ethel."

Too weak to protest, Mrs. Misrington allowed herself to be led through the gate and to a garden seat, while Maybelline ran for help. Mrs. Misrington inhaled the fresh clean scent of the garden, felt her chest expand and the sweat cool on her brow. "Oh my, but that smells good," she muttered.

As her breathing grew calmer, she looked around the patch and was jealously eyeing the garden when Maybee arrived with Tom. He carried a teapot and a cup of hot steaming tea on a tray.

"Try this," he offered soothingly.

"What is it?" Mrs. M grunted suspiciously.

"It's stinging nettle tea made of herbs known to help congestion. It'll fix you right up."

"We aren't here on a social call," Mrs. Misrington warned, reaching for the cup. She took a sip of tea and sighed a deep sigh.

Two cups later, the perk had returned to her ears, and her nose had gone from parched white to pink and moist again. But as soon as she stood up, she knew she'd never make it home in time. She bent and whispered urgently to her niece, "Maybelline, we have to go home this instant. I drank so much I have to tinkle."

Seeing that Auntie was about to wet her panties, Maybee quickly led her to the hut with the moon on the door.

"An outhouse! I told you these boys were backwards as cave men," Mrs. Misrington pronounced snootily.

"Hush, Aunt," whispered Maybee as she opened the door, and Mrs. M had no choice but to go in—to her immediate relief.

When she emerged from the outhouse, she was a new woman. She stood breathing the fragrant air and bathing her eyes in greenery, strangely full of kind and contented feelings.

"You boys need a proper flush toilet," she lectured Tom with only a hint of crankiness in her voice.

"It's a composting toilet, Auntie Ethel. Tom spreads the waste on his garden to feed the flowers."

Mrs. Misrington sniffed, horrified. "That is the most disgusting thing I have ever heard!"

Just then the pounding of a hammer rang through the air. Mrs. Misrington turned towards the sound and saw Oliver and Wilbur building something that looked like a bird house but larger and narrow with a slit in the bottom instead of a hole in the front. Suddenly it occurred to her.

Bat houses!

And wasn't that her wheelbarrow sitting over there filled with muck?

At once her blood pressure rose, and she remembered why she'd come in the first place.

"That's my wheelbarrow!" she cried, swatting at an annoying bee.

"Hello there, Maybee," Oli waved, not

noticing a raging Mrs. Misrington heading straight toward him. "Nice to see you again so soon."

"'...see you *again so soon*?!'" Mrs. M whirled on Maybee.

"Maybelline Burlingame Helena Stu! What on earth is the matter with you? Have you been fraternizing with these vermin?" She seized her niece by the arm and stared at her with burning eyes, a vein bulging in her forehead.

"Oh Auntie," Maybee began to cry.

"How could you? These Greens are a disgrace! They're dirty and backwards. They befriend bats and practice some kind of hocus pocus on their garden. Stay away from them! Hear me?"

Then turning on Oliver, Miz Biz screeched,

"Oliver 'Peeyew' Green—you are a common thief! That's my wheelbarrow. I knew all along you and your so-called brothers were thieving no-good do-gooders!"

Maybee tugged at her sleeve. "You're wrong!," she squeaked. "Oli, Will, and Tom are not bad rats. They're just trying to help Mother Nature by living simply and recycling whatever they can."

"'Help Mother Nature' my Aunt Fanny! They're trying to ruin the economy, that's what they're trying to do," Mrs. M raged, working herself into a quite a frenzy. At that very moment a realization popped into Maybee's brain—*her Auntie Ethel had not sneezed once since she stepped onto the Green's brother's patch!*

Oli, sweating and fidgeting nervously, didn't know what to do for that wheelbarrow did indeed come from Mrs. Misrington's trash pile.

Miz Biz kept right on shouting, "You boys stay away from my niece! She is none of your business. And stop putting bat houses up and down Broken Bottle Lane. Don't make me take steps, you hear? C'mon, Maybelline. We're leaving!"

Mad as a wet hen, she huffed and she puffed all the way home, dragging poor Maybee behind her.

Bumpity. Bumpity.

Bump.

Bump.

Bump.

That night Mrs. Ethel Misrington tossed and turned in her bed, thumped her pillow, and vowed, "I'm going to make those boys an offer they can't reuse!"

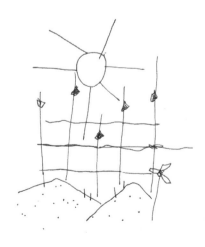

Cash Offers,
Nagging Violations

Early next morning, still shaken from the previous day's unpleasantness, Oliver decided that a nice round of junk hunting was just the ticket to settle his nerves. He wheeled his bike and trailer out the gate, and as he turned to close it, he saw a yellow paper tacked to it. Glancing around, he noticed the same yellow paper fluttering in the breeze on every gate up and down Broken Bottle Lane. It read:

CONGRATULATIONS!

Broken Bottle Lane has been chosen by
Rat Mart as the site of its first

Super Duper Big Box Store.

Every resident will receive $1,000 upon
signing this notice and handing it into
your nearest retail outlet.

Signed, Monty Bilko, Most Honorable
Mayor of Tintown,
on behalf of the Committee for
Tintown Big Business Development.

Everyone must sign.

P.S. Please vacate your property by
midnight tonight.

This set tongues to wagging all over Tintown.

"Wow! One thousand dollars!" enthused a wide-eyed waitress to every rat who came into the coffee shop.

"It's three times what my ramshackle patch is worth," the excited post office clerk shouted happily, waving his notice in the air and ignoring the line of rats waiting to buy stamps and post parcels.

"Where do I sign?" asked an elderly rat pulling a pen from the pocket of his frayed overcoat.

"No Way!" the three Greens thundered indignantly. *"It's our patch and nobody can make us leave!"*

The very next day Oli found a second, nastier notice plastered on their gate. It read:

VIOLATION!!!

Messrs. Green: It has come to our attention that you are in violation of the following codes:

(1) The Tintown zoning ordinance does not allow a compost heap.

(2) You don't have a permit for a windmill.

3) Chickens aren't allowed inside the city limits.

(4) Your grey-water tank is a health risk.

You will be fined $100 a day per violation until your patch complies with all Tintown codes, ordinances, and regulations. If you fail to comply within ten days, you must vacate the property.

Signed: Monty Bilko,
Tintown's Most Honorable Mayor

"One hundred dollars a day?" wailed Oli. "We don't have that kind of money!"

"We don't have any money. Zero," observed Wilbur, who was good at arithmetic.

"This patch has been in our family for generations. They're just trying to get rid of us so they can build that big box store. Oliver," Tom commanded, "where do you keep Grandpa's deed to the patch? Find it. We're going to City Hall."

So the three trekked in a pack down to the Tintown Town Hall to see what they could do.

8
Fiasco

"**O**h dear, I'm new here," purred the receptionist at the Tintown Town Hall. "Maybe you should speak to the town clerk. Down the hallway, to your right."

Oliver led the way, all three boys peering left and right at the gold lettering on each frosted glass door.

"Town clerk!" Wilbur pointed, and at once all three boys piled into the room.

The town clerk glanced at the two notices. "Hmm, a store. This is about zoning. Go to zoning."

"Where's zoning?"

"Down the hallway, to the right," the clerk snarled, reaching for his jangling phone.

After getting lost once, the boys arrived at the zoning department.

"Do you have proof of ownership for this patch?" inquired a crabby grey-haired she-rat with a dark and ominous glare.

"Yes!" chorused the brothers.

Tom turned to the other two. "The deed."

Will and Oli stared at him blankly then stared at each other until a light went on in Oliver's brain, and he commenced patting his pockets.

"Here!"

All three sighed with relief. Tom handed the ancient document to the zoning official who reached for her eyeglasses hanging on a cord around her neck. She studied the deed, carefully read every word of the official violation ticket, looked up at the boys, and pronounced, "This is an illegal eviction. We have bylaws against this sort of thing. Go to the lawyer in the legal department. It's down the hallway, to the right."

"Excuse me, Ma'am," Oli apologized to the

assistant's assistant seated inside the law-office door. "We need to see the lawyer."

"He's out to lunch," she yawned, nonchalantly cleaning her nails with the tip of a toothpick.

"How long will he be?" Tom asked, trying desperately to be polite.

"He usually takes three hours. Sometimes he doesn't come back at all. You'd better go see the sheriff. He enforces the law around here. Down the hallway, turn right."

"I can't help you!" the sheriff barked with a menacing sweep of his arm. "Ethel Misrington is my cousin. She would never break the law. I think you three forged this notice to blacken her name. I've a good mind to haul you in front of the judge for publishing scurrilous untruths. Constable, see that these three go straight to the judge."

They arrived just as the judge was closing the door of his chambers on his way to court. He listened impatiently to the constable's muddled version of events.

"It sounds to me like the sheriff imagines himself to be an expert in the law, which is not the case, I assure you. This is obviously

a matter for the Committee on Big Business Development, which the mayor heads. I suggest you take your grievance to Mayor Bilko directly. Go down this hall and turn right."

"I'm getting more worn out than a stack of bald tires at the dump," Oli sighed as he trudged down the hall to the mayor's office, Wilbur and Tom following glumly behind.

"Security! Security!" yelled the mayor as soon as he saw them. Two burly uniformed guards grabbed the boys by the scruffs of their necks and tossed them unceremoniously out of the building.

Thump

Thump

Thump

They landed at the foot of the cold cement steps—dazed, stunned, and completely befuddled.

Will dusted himself off and remarked disgustedly, "Well, that was a complete waste of ti—." But before he could finish his sentence, all three boys sniffed a change in the gravy cloud.

SMOKE!

9
FIRE!

Whoopwhoopwhoopwhoop.

Whoopwhoopwhoopwhoop.

Blaaast!

Whoopwhoopwhoop.

Fire trucks screeched by. Police cars rushed past, sirens bleating. Three pairs of alarmed yellow eyes followed the emergency vehicles.

"They're heading towards our patch," Will cried.

"Oh no!" they yelped, and took off at a sprint toward Broken Bottle Lane. The closer they got, the more deafening the noise, the more tangled the traffic, the more hectic the crowd. Rats poured out of buildings and onto the streets. Smoke thickened the already polluted Tintown air.

Oliver, Wilbur, and Tom pelted past scenes of chaos and confusion. Rats jostled and pushed, squabbled and screeched. Some gave advice whether anyone was listening or not. Others stood transfixed, and a few turned around and headed back to the safety of their huts.

As the boys skittered along, Oliver noticed cars slowing down. All at once everything ground to a halt in the most congested traffic jam Tintown had ever seen. Vehicles couldn't budge an inch. Fire trucks couldn't get through. Everything was stuck behind a big fat garbage truck mired in greasy sludge.

When the Greens squeezed past the garbage truck, they could see black smoke billowing over Broken Bottle Lane. That did it! As if propelled by supernatural powers, they leapt over the traffic jam, shouldered their way through the crowd, hopped over car bumpers, and squeezed

between pickup trucks until
they worked their
way around the
corner and onto their
beloved lane.

There, they saw
licks of fire leaping from
one stack of rubbish to the
next all along the alley in a
terrifying game of leapfrog.
They tore down the lane,
coughing in the smoke, when a gust
of hot, fire-fueled wind briefly shoved
the smoke aside.

They stopped short, falling over each other at
the sight of Tintown's fanciest house blazing like
a barbecue. There, in the driveway stood a soot-
covered Maybelline hopping up and down with
Mrs. Misrington's short garden hose in her tiny
hands, trying to make the trickle of water reach
all the way up to the second story.

The brothers looked up and saw Mrs.
Misrington in her baggy white undies hanging
precariously by her hands from her bedroom
balcony, one bony leg flailing to reach the railing.

"Heeeeeeeeeeeeeeelp meeeeee!"

"Mrs. Misrington!" Wilbur and Oli cried in unison.

"Maybee!" shouted Tom, his voice tense with fright. "Move. Get away from the house!"

Maybelline squeaked, "The stairs are on fire. Auntie can't get down. I've got to save her!"

"The hose!" Oliver hollered over the roar. "There's miles of it. We can hook it up to the grey-water tank."

Tom took Maybelline by the hand. "Come with us," he coaxed. "It's not safe here. We're going to get the hose. You'll be more use to your aunt if you help us."

Maybee's eyes widened with understanding. She turned and shouted up. "We're going to get the Greens' hose, Auntie. Hang on!"

"I am hanging on, you fool!"

They raced down the lane to the patch. Maybee flew quick as a jack rabbit and was already wrestling with the coil of hose and hooking one end up to the grey-water tank when the boys arrived. Even in the garden the air was hot and thick. Black smoke roiled menacingly through the treetops. Bats flew away in a panicked stream.

"Hurry!" Maybelline begged, dancing with agitation. Working smoothly together as if they'd been firemen all their lives, the boys stretched the hose across the lane. Maybelline ran ahead opening gates and directing the hose over walls, under fences, and through tight crevices until it reached Mrs. M's house. After feeding the hose through Mrs. Misrington's chain-link fence with just a few feet of hose to spare, Tom positioned himself directly in front of the flames.

"Help me! Help me! I'm stuck as a pig on a spit. I mean it Oliver, Wilbur, and Tom Green. Do not leave me here to roast," Mrs. Misrington screeched, her legs waving madly.

Tom turned to Maybee, "Okay girl, turn the water on *NOW!*"

Maybee flew down the lane onto the Greens' patch, pressed her hind paws against the grey-water tank, and cranked the faucet hard. Suddenly the hose jumped to life.

"Yes!" she cried and raced back faster than

water could run through the hose. She arrived just in time to see Tom catapulting into the air as a jet of water shot straight out at Mrs. Misrington. A glorious arc of dirty washwater knocked her back in the window and washed her all the way down the stairs and out the front door.

Whoosh!

Plop!

Maybee ran and flung her arms around her aunt's neck. "Auntie, we saved you!"

"Hack, hack, hack," Mrs. M sputtered, coughing up goo. "I ripped my underpants," she sobbed, rivulets of tears staining her sooty face. Looking at her disheveled wet clothes now tinged with grey she sputtered, "What is this disgusting stuff?"

"Grey water, ma'am," Oliver said proudly.

Mrs. Ethel Misrington staggered to her feet and turned around to face the pile of soggy ash that only an hour ago was her home. "My house," she wailed. "My epilator, my automatic pillow press, my plasma screen, my spyware, my nighttime vermin vision goggles—all my ratopia gone to rubble!"

"But Auntie Ethel, what about YOU? You're still here."

Mrs. Misrington couldn't deny that. So she pulled herself up, took a deep breath to clear her smoky lungs, and croaked to the boys, "Well, I'm mighty thankful for the rescue."

Just then the mayor arrived huffing and puffing for he had to leave his limousine way back in the traffic jam and find his way on foot. He hurried over to Mrs. Misrington exclaiming,

"Dear Ethel. How dreadful." Putting his arm around her shoulders, Mayor Bilko turned to the onlookers and pronounced with authority, "We'll find the varmints responsible for this."

It was all too much for Mrs. Misrington. She put her snout in her paws and whined, "I'm so humiliated you're seeing me in this state of undress." Despite themselves, Maybee and Mayor Bilko looked down at Mrs. M's baggy grey undies. Though wet and dirty, you could clearly see the embroidered letters enclosed in a pink, chain-stitched heart.

The mysterious letters on the stamped hearts! Could they stand for Ethel Misrington and Monty Bilko? The mayor appeared to have the same thought, for his eyes suddenly brightened with emotion.

"Does this mean," he pointed to the embroidery, "that you still care?"

"Oh Monty, YES! I do!" She affirmed, hiding her tears in his right honorable shoulder.

The mayor took off his jacket and gallantly wrapped it around her shoulders.

A cheering crowd quickly gathered around the seriously soiled brothers.

Whoop whoop.

Emergency vehicles finally arrived and firemen leapt off the truck.

"You're too late! These guys put it out already," someone shouted.

"Yeah, go find your own fire," sniggered two lanky teenage rats.

The firemen looked a tad embarrassed but swarmed into the house with their axes anyway.

"You boys are heroes," yelled a grateful Tintowner.

"If it weren't for you, the fire would have burnt up the whole lane!" announced a young mother, clutching her four ratlings.

"I'd have preferred clean water," complained someone else.

Just then, the fire marshal clomped out of the wreckage, holding up a frayed electrical cord. "Here's what started the fire," he said peering meaningfully at Mrs. Misrington with one eyebrow arched. "Somebody plugged a refrigerator, a computer, a toaster, a microwave, a food processor, an air conditioner, and an electric iron into this extension cord then plugged the whole thing into a single socket. It was too much. It all went kaflooey."

"She got what she deserved then," a cranky rat called out as grumbles of agreement rustled through the crowd.

"You really should live a better way," Maybee whispered into her aunt's singed ear. Mrs. M's puffed-up persona shrank and shivered.

The mayor patted her arm, then scrambled up onto the back of the fire truck and, summoning his best orator's voice, addressed the crowd.

"I can assure you there will be a full investigation. In the meantime, join me at the Tintown Town Hall at noon o'clock tomorrow to honor these brave brothers who saved Broken Bottle Lane—indeed, the whole of Tintown—from certain destruction."

10

Hip Hip Hooray

Next morning Oliver took the longest bath of his life. He even washed between his toes and behind his ears.

Dressed in their cleanest duds, the boys took off for the Tintown Town Hall where they were amazed to find that, instead of red tape, a red carpet welcomed them. The security guards who had thrown them out the day before bowed respectfully as the boys climbed the steps. All around them news cameras flashed, and reporters shouted questions.

"We're willing to pay for an exclusive interview," an eager journalist thrust a contract into Wilbur's hands.

"It's doable," Will responded, not the least bit perturbed, for he had always been certain that an original inventor like himself would be recognized one day.

"So nice to see you," the receptionist greeted with a humble smile.

The sheriff sucked in his flabby belly, thrust out his chest, and saluted smartly before escorting the brothers into the Great Hall, where all of Tintown awaited. As soon as the Greens came through the door, eight trumpets blared out a fanfare and eight snare drums rolled out a smart tattoo.

As they moved up the aisle to the stage, everyone clamored to shake their paws. Wilbur turned and waved at the crowd in the manner of visiting royalty.

"Gosh," muttered Oliver. "It's taking us as long to see the mayor today as it did when we were on the wrong side of the law."

Seated in rows beneath the stage, the Tintown High School Marching Band played the only two tunes they knew over and over again, their young ears perking up on either side of braided peaked caps.

On the stage sat all the members of the Tintown Town Council, as well as other prominent citizens, including Mrs. Misrington who was clearly enjoying the pomp and hoopla. She seemed to have recovered from the

previous day's humiliation and stood straight as a pin proudly wearing clothes borrowed that very morning from Mayor Bilko's sister.

Beside her, bouncing in her seat and beaming with pride, little Maybelline Burlingame Helena Stu sat all gussied up in a white dress with a gauzy skirt embroidered with pink silk rosettes. Now actually big enough to climb onto a grownup's chair, she waved and swung her pink patent-leather slippers in the air, for her feet did not yet reach the floor.

Wilbur, Tom, and Oliver smiled and waved back as they neared the stage. Before they could take another step forward, one more trumpet blast assaulted their ears, and the clerk bellowed, "All rise for His Honor, Mayor Monty Bilko."

The hall reverberated with shuffling, scraping, and muttering as the crowd rose to its feet. Mayor Bilko, resplendent in his robes and chain of office, crossed the stage and took his seat on a carved chair behind the podium.

The town clerk motioned the three brothers forward as the mayor stepped up to the microphone to announce, "Our guests of honor have arrived!" But his voice was immediately drowned out by earsplitting feedback. Everyone in the hall squeezed their eyes shut and covered their ears.

"Ladies and gentle-rats," the mayor began. "We are gathered together today to honor three extraordinary citizens born and bred in our fair city: Oliver, Wilbur, and Tom Green."

At the mention of their names, the audience broke into hoots, hollers, and deafening applause.

"With courage, bravery, foresight, and a whole lot of grey water, they have taught us all a valuable lesson. We now know we must change our ways or destroy ourselves in the process." He turned to the three smiling Green brothers and continued, "In their own way, day by day, they are making Tintown a cleaner place with a slower pace, like it used to be years ago when we were just ratlings. For that, we the citizens of Tintown bestow upon them the Tintown Medal of Honor. Three cheers for our heroes," the mayor bellowed, grinning from ear to ear.

"Hip hip hooray!

Hip hip hooray!

Hip hip hooray!"

shouted every last Tintowner as they broke into wild applause.

The mayor pinned a gleaming tin medal on the front of Oli's clean, striped shirt, an identical one on the broad lapel of Will's coat, and one on the strap of Tom's overalls. For once Mayor Bilko didn't mind getting close to Oliver who smelled as fresh as eucalyptus that day and looked spiffier than anyone had ever seen him.

"Speech! Speech!" demanded the crowd as the mayor ushered Wilbur to the podium. An expectant hush fell over the room.

Wilbur, who only moments before basked in the attention, stood stunned as a rabbit caught in headlights. For the first time in his life he couldn't think of a word to say.

Oliver stepped up to speak in his place, but when he leaned into the microphone, he found his courage had deserted him as well. He turned and looked pleadingly at Tom.

So it fell to shy, retiring Tom, who had never addressed more than three rats at once, to deliver the most important speech in the history of Tintown. He smiled at Maybee, took a deep breath, and spoke from his heart.

"Look around, citizens. You are knee-deep in your own trash, held captive by technology, and so caught up in the rat race you don't have time to think." He paused to collect his thoughts.

"We are ruining our corner of Mother Earth, creating a place where no living being can thrive. We've cut down our trees, poisoned our air, and dumped sewage in our rivers and streams. It's time to step back and ask ourselves, 'Is this what we really want for our children?' We must learn to live simply. We must walk softly upon Mother Earth and stop taking more than we need to survive."

"*Yessiree!*" shouted a clean-cut rat from the back of the room.

"Right on!" yelled Marge, the diner waitress, waving her apron in the air.

"We can make it happen!" shouted first one citizen, then another, until it became a chant.

With all the positive energy in the room Wilbur plucked up his courage and stepped up to speak into the microphone.

"Each one one of you can earn a medal just like this one," he began, pointing to the shiny circle on his lapel. "We must learn to help each other, for that is the secret to a happy life. Let us put aside our differences, put the neighbor back in 'hood,' and work together to create a world that honors nature."

"*Yes! Yes! Yes!*" murmured the crowd in a wave of understanding.

Suddenly, someone in the front of the crowd shouted, "Hey Mayor, what are you and the town council going to do besides stand up there in your fancy clothes and hand out medals?"

It was the reporter who'd asked Wilbur for an exclusive. He was holding up his palm-sized recording device, and a photographer flashed a photo.

The Mayor thrust out his chest and forced a smile. "Well, we'll... we'll...we'll..." he turned to the town council and whispered, "What will we do?"

Before any of them could come up with an answer, Mrs. Misrington rose from her chair and walked to the podium. "I know what I'm going to do. Instead of building a Super Rat Mart, I'm pledging my money towards setting up a ...," unsure of her wording, she turned to Maybelline.

Her niece ran over to join her aunt. Someone rushed over with a chair for Maybee to stand on so she could see over the top of the podium. "...Setting up a Refresh, Renew, Regenerate Foundation with the mission of charting a path for a better tomorrow," she said, hastily finishing her aunt's sentence.

"*Hooray! Hooray!*" shouted the crowd, tossing their hats, purses, and baby ratlings in the air.

"The foundation includes sponsorship

of the Walk Softly Community School for Ecological Understanding. Oliver," Maybelline smiled at him, "will show us how to get the best use out of everything we ordinarily throw away. Wilbur can teach the basics of water conservation and energy efficiency. Tom will show us how to make compost and stop using industrial chemicals on our gardens, for that is the secret to his prize-winning tomatoes."

Astonished, Mrs. Misrington looked at her and thought, "How did all those big words get into that little head? This niece of mine may not be able to run a retail empire, but I know who'll be running my foundation when she grows up. I wonder if this foundation will be good for business."

"Hooray! Hooray!" shouted the crowd again and again.

So, led by Tintown's modest heroes, the newly invigorated citizens of Tintown set about living in a sustainable way, nurturing the earth and all its creatures.

They continue to do so today, reducing and reusing and recycling every chance they get (which is nearly all the time). Today, Tintown is a cleaner, quieter place with a slower pace, just like it used to be years ago.

Well, you know the rest, for nobody wants to live in a gravy cloud if they don't have to.

Those crazy enough to think they can change the world are the ones who do.

The End

For more rat fun go to
www.threegreenrats.com

"Whatever you can dream you can do. Begin it. Boldness has genius, power, and magic in it. Begin it now."

— *Goethe, 1749-1832*

Glossary

befuddle: Unable to think clearly

callous: Insensitive and cruel disregard for others

canny: Having shrewdness, especially when it comes to money or business

cistern: An underground reservoir for holding water

chartreuse: A pale green or yellow color

coiffed: An elaborate hairstyle

compact: Closely and neatly packaged together

compost: Decayed organic material (vegetable or manure) used as plant fertilizer

composting toilet: A human waste disposal system consisting of a toilet that uses little or no water connected to a specially built tank in which waste material decomposes, producing good fertilizer for nonedible plants

cottonwoods: A tall tree found in North America

dahlia: Pronounced *dal-ya*. A showy type of flower

decompose: Decay; become rotten

diligent: Having care with one's work or duties

din: Bedlam, boisterousness, disquiet

dishevel: In disarray; disorder

domestic: Of or relating to the running of a home

eave: The projecting overhang at the lower
   edge of a roof

eccentric: Odd behavior, as opposed to "normal"

ecological: The interdependence of living
   organisms in an environment

emerald: Bright green in color

epilater: An electrical appliance for plucking
   unwanted hair

eucalyptus: A fast-growing evergreen tree of
   the myrtle family. The sweet-smelling oil
   from eucalyptus leaves has medicinal properties.

fertilizer: Any substance added to soil or water
   to increase its productivity. Organic fertilizer
   is made up of animal or vegetable matter.

forage: To search widely

generator: A machine for converting mechanical
   energy into electricity

glossary: A list of words

grey: A neutral tone between black and white

grey-water: Leftover water from baths,
   showers, hand basins, and washing machines
   only. Some definitions of grey-water include
   water from the kitchen sink. Any water
   containing human waste is considered black
   water. Grey-water can be recycled on-site for
   uses such as landscape irrigation.

Goethe, Johann Wolfgang von (1749-18), German poet and scientist; one of the greatest figures in European literature.

gussied up: To put on special clothes to appear particularly appealing and attractive

infestigate: A word Maybee made up

haunt: To visit often, or appear in the form of a ghost

hedges: Neatly trimmed bushes

humus: The end result of compost. A brown or black organic substance consisting of partially or wholly decayed vegetable or animal matter that provides nutrients for plants and increases the ability of soil to retain water.

harrumph: A noisy clearing of the throat

HopRod: A motorized pogo stick; actually exists.

imperceptible: Impossible or difficult to perceive by the mind or senses

Jaguar: A very expensive sports car named after a large heavily-built cat found in the forests of Central and South America

lacquer: A hard protective coating

lavendar bush: A small aromatic evergreen shrub of the mint family, with narrow leaves and bluish-purple flowers

manicure: A cosmetic treatment of the fingernails, including shaping and polishing

mayhem: Chaos, confusion, disorder

messrs.: An abbreviation for the French word *"messieurs"* which means men.

mosaic: A picture or decoration made of small, usually colored pieces of inlaid stone or glass

nettle: An herb; a specific plant used for medicine, usually congestion

nutrient: Providing nourishment

nurture: To care for; to encourage the development of

oak: Any tree or shrub bearing the acorn as fruit

obstinacy: Being stubborn

perky: Lively, enthusiastic

perpetual: Lasting a long time

persona: The aspect of someone's character that is presented to or perceived by others

pesticide: A substance used for destroying insects or other organisms harmful to cultivated plants or to animals. Can be synthetic (toxic chemicals made in a laboratory) or organic (plant-based).

pivot: The act of turning

plucked up courage: The power of facing danger

pollen: A fine powdery substance, typically yellow, of microscopic grains discharged from the male part of a flower or plant

pollinate: To fertilize a plant or flower with pollen

precocious: Having developed certain abilities or proclivities at an earlier age than usual

putrid: A rotten smell

ramshackle: Dilapidated, decrepit, rickety

replenish: To make whole again; to complete

scurrilous: Pronounced *skur-a-les*. Vulgar, evil

solar panel: A panel designed to absorb the sun's rays for generating electricity or heating

sustain: To keep up or keep going

sustainable: Capable of being continued with minimal long-term effect on the environment

tatoo: (1.) A drumroll. (2.) To mark a person or part of the body with an indelible design by inserting pigment into punctures in the skin.

transfixed: Cause someone to become motionless with horror, wonder, or astonishment

trek: To journey on foot

unconventional: Not what is generally done or believed

unison: Happening at the same time

With Gratitude

To Cynthia Nugent, our editor, for pulling our little story together with humor and finesse.

To Natalie Hawryshkewich who matched words to pictures, and to Joline Rivera who made the layout sing.

To Iris Albina who with astute professionalism proofread our little book, and to Roberta Kim Summersgill for offering suggestions.

To David Stephens who introduced us to Kafka.

To Charlotte Kwon who helped us more than she will ever know with one simple email.

To Friesen's for printing in a sustainable manner. In a better world, this wouldn't be so hard to find.

To our parents who gave us our childhoods.

To our husbands who endured and listened, listened and endured, and supported us throughout.

Thank You.